Small
in the
City

Sydney Smith

NEAL PORTER BOOKS
HOLIDAY HOUSE/NEW YORK

Neal Porter Books

Text and illustrations copyright © 2019 by Sydney Smith
All Rights Reserved
HOLIDAY HOUSE is registered in the U.S. Patent and Trademark Office.
Printed and bound in February 2019 at Toppan Leefung, DongGuan City, China.
The artwork for this book was created using ink, watercolor, and a bit of gouache.
Book design by Jennifer Browne
www.holidayhouse.com
First Edition
1   3   5   7   9   10   8   6   4   2

Library of Congress Cataloging-in-Publication Data

Names: Smith, Sydney, 1980– author, illustrator.
Title: Small in the city / Sydney Smith.
Description: First edition. | New York : Holiday House, [2019] | "Neal Porter
Books." | Summary: A little boy offers advice to his cat, which is lost
in the city, from taking shortcuts through safe alleys to finding a friend
in the park.
Identifiers: LCCN 2018042402 | ISBN 9780823442614 (hardcover)
Subjects: | CYAC: City and town life—Fiction. | Cats—Fiction. | Lost and
found possessions—Fiction.
Classification: LCC PZ7.1.S6566 Sm 2019 | DDC [E]—dc23 LC record available
at https://lccn.loc.gov/2018042402

This book is dedicated to the memory of Sheila Barry.

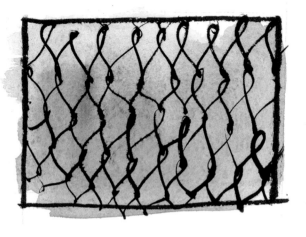

People don't see you and loud sounds can scare you,

and knowing
what to do is
hard sometimes.

Taxis honk their horns.

Sirens come and go
in every direction.

Construction sites pound
and drill and yell and dig.

The streets are always busy.

It can make your brain feel like
there's too much stuff in it.

But I know you.
You'll be all right.
If you want, I can give you
some advice.

Alleys can be good shortcuts.

But don't go down this alley.
It's too dark.

Three big dogs chase and
bite each other in this yard.
I would avoid the place . . .

if I were you.

There are lots of
good places to hide,
like under this mulberry bush.

Or up the black walnut tree.

There is a dryer vent that
breathes out hot steam that smells
like summer.

You could curl up
below it and have a nap.

The fishmongers down the street
are nice.

They would probably give you
a fish if you asked.

This empty lot looks like a
good place to rest, but the bushes
have burrs.

They might get stuck
to your coat.

I know you like to listen to music.

In the blue house down the street
someone's always playing piano,
and there is a choir that
practices in the red brick church.

You could perch on the window ledge.

In the park I have a favorite bench.
Sometimes my friend is there.

If you see her, say hi.
You could sit on her lap
and she will pet you.

But home is safe and quiet.

Your food dish is full and your
blanket is warm.

If you want,
you could just come back.

But I know you.

You will be all right.